The Chest of Tools

By Madeline Leslie

NATAL PUBLISHING LLC
ARS LONGA, VITA BREVIS

CHAPTER I.

THE CUT FINGERS.

MR. DRAKE was at work upon his carpenter's bench when he heard an angry scream; and then a shriek of distress from two boys, who were at play in the lower part of the shop.

One of the boys was his son Henry, the other, his nephew Ernest Monroe. He waited a moment to see whether the cry would be continued, when he was startled by hearing Henry exclaim,—

"O father! Come, come quick! Ernest has cut himself dreadfully."

The children were standing before an open tool chest, which Mr. Drake had often forbidden them to meddle with. In the midst of his fright, his anger was excited that they had dared to disobey him, and he called out, in a harsh voice,—

"Boys, how came my tool chest open? Which of you presumed to unlock it?"

Henry and Ernest were both silent. Henry dared not confess the truth, and his cousin, even if he had wished to tell tales, was at that moment too faint to speak. Indeed, just before his uncle reached him, he fell prostrate among the shavings that covered the floor.

"Why! Why! What does this mean?" exclaimed the carpenter, now seriously alarmed.

Then seeing the pool of blood, which had streamed from Ernest's poor, cut fingers, he caught up the child, and stepping over a low wall which separated his own from his sister's grounds, soon laid him pale and unconscious on his own bed.

"We must have the doctor here as soon as we can get him," he said, in an excited tone, "or Ernest's hand will be useless. Henry, what are you gaping round here for? Why, you ought to be half way to the doctor's!"

Mrs. Monroe trembled from head to foot; but, rallying very soon, she proceeded to make an examination of the wound. Though covered with blood, it was easy to see that three fingers of the right hand were cut to the bone; besides a bad gash in the palm.

She washed off the blood as well as she could, and then held the fingers in place, keeping them warm within her own, till the physician arrived.

The cut was so deep, the doctor found it necessary to take a few stitches in each finger, and then, having bandaged them, he gave the boy a soothing powder, and left, promising to call the next day.

All this time his uncle sat by, his face growing hard and stern. As soon as he perceived that Ernest could speak, he began,—

"Now I want to know how this happened. Who has dared to unlock my tool chest against my positive orders?"

"Stop, brother," said Mrs. Monroe, firmly, at the same time interposing herself between the carpenter and his nephew. "Ernest is too weak now to talk. When he is better, I will ask him all about it."

"But, Jane, it's a pretty business if I can't lock up my tool chest without the risk of having a lot of careless boys meddling with my things. There's my new adze I saw lying on the floor and covered with blood. I dare say it's spoiled, and—"

"John, you heard the doctor say Ernest must be quiet. If you will talk, come in here."

The boy heard a few loud, angry words from his uncle, and then the door was shut.

"Try to go to sleep," said his mother, bending over him and softly kissing his cheek.

"Yes, ma'am," faltered the boy; "but I do wish Henry would tell his father the truth."

"Would it make you feel easier, to tell me about it, now?"

Ernest sighed. "I did naughty, mother; but I didn't unlock Uncle John's tool chest. I began to play with the tools, though. The new adze was as sharp as a razor, Henry said; and so we tried cutting a hair with it. Henry did it twice, and then it was my turn; but he liked the fun, and wouldn't let me have it; so I tried to snatch it away, and I cut my fingers."

"I'm very sorry, indeed, my dear boy. But did Henry unlock the chest?"

"That was another naughty thing, I did, mother; I promised not to tell anybody. You know I tell you most everything; but this time I forgot."

"Well, Ernest, it is a sad affair; but we wont talk any more about it this morning. You'll feel stronger after you've had a nap."

She drew down the curtain at the foot of his bed, and, leaving the door ajar, went back to her morning work. Twice she crept to the bedroom, and peeped through the crack, and at last, finding him to be asleep, shut the door and left him.

CHAPTER II.

HENRY'S LIE.

IT was nearly noon when she heard a sound of voices in the bedroom. She wondered who could have gone there without her knowledge, and stopped outside the door to listen.

The visitor was Henry, and he was saying angrily,—

"No, you sha'n't. You promised certain true, black and blue, you wouldn't tell anybody. If Aunt Jane knows it, she'll tell father; and he'll half kill me. He's awful angry now."

"But, Henry," urged Ernest half crying, "he'll think I stole the key out of his pocket; and I didn't. It's too bad, if I have to have my fingers cut, and bear all the blame, too, when you did it. My cut smarts awfully."

Mrs. Monroe now made a noise to let them know she was near, and then opened the door, just in season to see Henry raise the window, and jump out.

"Ah!" said the lady to herself. "That's the way he came in without my seeing him."

"Have you been awake long, Ernest?" asked his mother.

"Henry waked me, getting in through the window. I wish he'd stayed away. He's made my head ache so."

"I've made you some milk porridge, dear; I'll bring you a cupful; and then perhaps you'll fall asleep again. I'll lock the window this time."

Ernest drank his favorite porridge; but he could not sleep. Henry's words were constantly recurring to his mind. "If you tell, father 'll half kill me. He's awful angry now."

Ernest was a timid boy, not tough and hearty, like his cousin, but feeble from his infancy; "only raised to the age of eleven years," as the doctor said, "by the unwearied nursing of a good mother."

Ernest had a great dread of his uncle's rough word's and hot temper, very different from the manners of his own parents. One time and another, from being a constant companion of his cousin, he had experienced a good deal of harsh treatment from the carpenter. Now he lay, tossing and turning his head on the pillow, thinking of Henry's words, wondering whether he could be induced to confess, and dreading his uncle's wrath.

At noon, when his father, who was a clock-maker, came home to his dinner, after hearing the story from his wife, he found his son's face burning with fever.

"O pa!" exclaimed the boy. "I'm so glad you've come. Is it ever right to break a promise?"

"That depends, my boy, on what kind of a promise it is. Suppose I, to escape an assassin, should promise a wicked man that I would help him murder his neighbor; ought I therefore to keep the promise?"

Ernest shook his head thoughtfully.

"Then, again," added Mr. Monroe, "if a boy were placed so that he were obliged to promise to do what he did not approve, to save his life, for instance, I think such a promise ought not to be binding."

"But suppose, pa, that a boy forgot, and promised he wouldn't tell something, when he had promised before that he would tell his mother everything he did; what would God want him to do?"

"You needn't worry yourself about that, Ernest," said his mother, coming into the room. "I know all you want to tell me; I know that Henry stole from his father's pocket the key of the tool chest and opened it."

"Did Henry tell you! Oh, I'm so glad!"

"I can't say how I learned it; but you may rest about your uncle's displeasure."

Ernest burst out crying.

"I was afraid Henry 'd make him think I did it; and he'd whip me, I know he would. He don't know what he's doing when he gets angry."

"If he dares to lay a finger on you," exclaimed the father, rising, "I'll have the law on him."

"Hush," said Mrs. Monroe, soothingly; "there is no danger; your fever has excited you, Ernest, and you must have some drops. How should you like to have me bring my work, and sit here this afternoon? Or perhaps I'll tell you a story."

"I'd like it first-rate."

"Well, I'll hurry and get through with my work. Do you want a piece of custard pie?"

"I don't want to eat anything, my head aches so."

CHAPTER III.

THE LIE FOUND OUT.

"THE moment I can leave work, I'll go to the shop, and have a talk with John," said Mr. Monroe, after they had for some time been seated at the table.

"No, I wouldn't," mildly said his wife. "I'm going to have a talk with Henry. It would be a great deal better to get him to confess."

"Henry is growing to be a bad boy. I wish they didn't live so near. Sometimes I think we shall have to sell our place. I don't want Ernest to associate with such a boy. Then everything that's lost or out of place is laid to our child, whether he ever saw it or not. I'm sick of living so."

"We cannot move away from trials, let us go where we will," was the pleasant reply. "Generally John is a good neighbor, and his wife I love dearly. Besides, Henry is unfortunate in being so afraid of his father, and would be worse than he is, if it wasn't for Ernest."

By this time, Mr. Monroe had finished his second piece of custard pie, and rose from the table with a smile, saying,—

"Well, Jane, have it your own way. You're generally right. 'Blessed are the peace-makers,' the Saviour says; and I'm sure you've made peace between John and me a score of times."

In the afternoon, when the mother was ready to sit by Ernest, he had fallen asleep again. His face was very pale, and, as she bent over him, her heart went up to God in prayer, that, if it was God's will that he should be weak in body, his head might be strong to resist evil; that he might be gathered into the fold of the good Shepherd.

Then she sat down close to the window, and presently she saw her brother's wife, stepping over the wall, on her way to the house. She went out to the sitting-room, softly closing the door behind her.

"I'm really sorry about Ernest," Mary Anne exclaimed, falling into the rocking chair, with a sigh. "Does Doctor Frost think he can save the hand?"

"Oh, yes, he hopes to! The only danger is that the muscles, which were cut quite off, will contract. I am hopeful, for I cut my finger once when a child, and for months had no use of it. But constant trying brought it round at last. See, it's as useful a finger as I have now." And she held up her forefinger for notice.

"What does he say about it?"

"He says he did not unlock the chest."

"That's true, Jane; I know he didn't."

The mother looked pleased.

"Oh, dear!" sighed Mary Anne. "If John wasn't so hot, I could set it all right, but,—well it's no use to cry-about what never will be different. I was making the beds when I heard Henry creep upstairs to the closet where his father hangs his clothes. I was going to ask him what he wanted when he said,—

"'Goody, here 'tis now!'

"He went down, and I heard the jingle of keys."

Mrs. Monroe then repeated the conversation, she had overheard between the boys, and added, "I do wish Henry would tell his father."

"Yes, he ought, but I don't believe he'll dare to. He has told ever so many lies already; for, when his father asked him, he said he was going along by the chest and he saw it open.

"'How came Ernest by my new adze?' John asked.

"I don't know, sir. I saw him with it, and told him to put it down; he wouldn't, and so I tried to make him. That's how he got cut.'

"It's dreadful for Henry to tell such falsehoods," said his aunt, shaking her head. "I'd much rather have Ernest cut his fingers, than to act so wickedly."

"I don't mean it as an excuse, of course," urged his mother; "but if John were like your husband, 'twould be easier for Henry to tell the truth."

"Mother, mother!" called out the sick boy.

Mrs. Monroe led the way to the bedroom, where she was followed by her sister-in-law.

"Where's Henry, Aunt Mary Anne? I want to see him," eagerly exclaimed Ernest.

"He's at work clearing the shop floor of shavings. His father has set him to do it."

"When he's done, please ask him to come here."

"Yes, I will."

"There is nothing that hardens the heart so much as lying," said Mrs. Monroe, "one lie leads on to another, until there is no knowing where it will end. I remember my mother used to say, 'There is no safety except in perfect truthfulness.'"

"Don't you believe I have told the truth, mother?" said Ernest, looking up at her inquiringly, as he spoke.

"Yes, Ernest, I do; and so does your aunt."

"I have never caught Ernest in a lie," said Mrs. Drake, sighing again. "If I had, I never should trust you again."

"It's hard sometimes to tell the truth right off," began the boy; "but it is a great deal harder to wait."

CHAPTER IV.

ANOTHER LIE.

"WE'VE been in to Mrs. Monroe's to see Ernest," said Mrs. Drake, when she was seated at the supper-table. "He looks as if he had lost a good deal of blood."

"Well, the young rascal deserves to suffer; it may save him from the gallows."

Henry shuddered, but did not speak.

"What do you mean?" inquired his wife.

"Mean!" he repeated the words in an angry tone. "Why, if it has come to this, that my pockets are picked, my trunks unlocked, and my tools ruined by a scamp of a boy, it's time something was done about it,—that's all! If I caught my boy in such tricks, I'd whip him within an inch of his life."

Henry's eyes were fastened, on his plate. If he had ever had an idea of confessing that he, instead of his cousin, was the guilty boy, it vanished at once.

When he had finished his supper, his mother told him that Ernest wished to see him. When he had left the room, she said,—

"I do wish, John, you wouldn't talk so strong. Don't you see that if Henry were to disobey you, he wouldn't dare to tell you of it. It seems to me, parents ought to show their children that if they are really penitent, they will be forgiven."

"I don't know what you're driving at, wife; but if it's anything about the tools, you may stop hinting. Just as soon as Ernest is out of bed. I'll haul him over the coals as sure as my name is John Drake. I never forgive, as you have learned long ago."

"Don't you remember the verse, that Maria repeated at the concert, which the minister explained so beautifully? 'If ye forgive men their trespasses, your heavenly Father will also forgive you; but if ye forgive not men their trespasses, neither will your Father in heaven forgive your trespasses.'"

Knocking the ashes out of his pipe, Mr. Drake went out without answering.

His wife, with a heavy heart, began to collect the plates, when Henry burst into the room.

His cheeks burned like fire, and he was evidently excited; but as he volunteered no explanation, his mother, after a glance at him, went on with her work.

The truth is that both his Aunt Jane and Ernest had been urging him to tell his father what he had done. At first, he tried to hide his confusion by more lies, repeating the story he had told his father about finding the chest open. But Ernest exclaimed with such evident horror,—"O Henry! You told me you found the key in his pants' pocket," that he found it was no use to go on.

"If you don't tell, I'm afraid I must," said his aunt, firmly. "Ernest shall not suffer from your fault. It was very wrong of him to touch the tools when he knew that his uncle had forbidden it. If the adze is injured, he must take his spending money, and buy a new one. I'm afraid Henry, you don't realize what a wicked thing it is to tell a lie."

"I'm sorry I ever touched the old chest," exclaimed Henry, in a passionate tone. "I wouldn't if Ernest hadn't teased me to. I never should have thought of hunting up the key if he hadn't put it into my head."

"Stop, Henry; you are only adding sin to sin. The Bible says: 'All liars shall have their portion in the lake that burns with fire and brimstone.' If you are afraid to confess on account of your father's anger, why do you not fear the wrath of God, who knows every thought of your heart?"

Henry went to bed that night feeling that, turn which way he would, he was in trouble.

"If I tell father," he said to himself, "he'll half kill me; and if I don't, he'll find it out by Aunt Jane; and there 'll be a dreadful row."

The good Spirit whispered to him,—

"You have sinned. Confess your fault, and accept the punishment you deserve. Your heart will then be at rest."

But Henry would not listen to the good Spirit. He said to himself,—

"If I stick to my lie, he'll believe me sooner than he will Ernest; 'cause when he once gets an idea in his head, he wont give it up nohow. He thinks Ernest did it, and I—guess—I'll—let—him—think—so."

CHAPTER V.

THE BROKEN KNIFE.

SCHOOL commenced again the beginning of the week; but Ernest was not in his place. He was a good scholar, obedient to the rules of the school, and therefore a great favorite With his teacher.

"Henry Drake, do you know why Ernest Monroe isn't here?" she asked, when the class to which he belonged came out to recite.

"He's sick, ma'am."

"I must go and see him," said the teacher.

After recess, she learned the story as it was told by Henry to the scholars.

"Ernest stole father's keys, unlocked his tool chest, and cut his hand with a new adze."

"That does not sound true. I wont believe such a story till Ernest tells me himself," said the lady. "I'll call at Mrs. Monroe's on my way home."

She did call; and Henry, who saw her enter the house, slunk away feeling very much like a thief.

The next half hour was a very pleasant one to the sick boy. He frankly confessed to his teacher his fault; but when she asked who unlocked the chest, answered,—

"Mother knows. I'd rather not tell anybody else."

"Well," said the lady, rising at last to leave. "You must hurry and get well; for my first class miss you sadly. Can't you have your books at home, and keep up with the lessons?"

"Yes, ma'am. I should like it. Mother can hear me every day."

At the end of a fortnight, Ernest was in his desk, looking rather thin to be sure, but pleased to be back in school. His right hand hung in a sling, and his companions were very careful the half-healed fingers should receive no injury by their carelessness.

To the surprise of some of his class, Ernest went on with the lesson, which happened to be review, as if he had not been absent a day. At the close of the recitation in spelling, he unexpectedly found himself at the head of his class.

"Mother and I had a school at home," he exclaimed joyfully to his teacher at recess. "We took turns in hearing the class recite. She said I was very strict."

At the end of another week, the teacher one afternoon told her pupils to lay aside their books as she wished to talk to them.

"Two days ago," she began, "I lost a little knife, with a pearl handle. I used it in my desk, and felt quite sure I left it here; but, after searching in vain, outside and inside the desk, I made up my mind I had taken it home in my pocket by mistake. I would not suspect one of my scholars of so mean a thing as borrowing my knife without leave; and I dared not for a moment entertain the thought that any one here would steal from the teacher.

"I looked for it at home without success; but what was my surprise this afternoon, when I opened my desk, to find the knife lying directly before me, the blade broken so badly that it was useless!"

She held up the knife, while her eye glanced rapidly from one scholar to another.

All were very curious; some expressed indignation at the deed; but no one seemed particularly moved except Ernest Monroe. His usually pale cheeks were dyed with blushes, while tears trembled in his eyes, and he covered his face.

"What can it mean," thought the teacher. "I'm sure Ernest is not the guilty one; and yet he looks so embarrassed."

"Can any of you tell me how my knife came to be broken?" asked Miss Fosdick. "I will readily forgive the offender if she or he will confess. It is a wicked thing to steal; don't add to the sin by a lie. Come up to the desk bravely, and tell me the whole truth."

No one moved, but several of the scholars noticed how much Ernest tried to hide his confusion. He opened and shut his desk, and held his face closely over his books.

"Don't he look guilty?" whispered Henry Drake, touching his companion under the seat.

"Ernest," Miss Fosdick said at last, "have you nothing to say to me?"

"No, ma'am." And then, to the surprise of the whole school, the little boy began to cry, sobbing as if his heart would break.

Ernest was known to be a favorite. Most of his companions thought he deserved to be so; but now there were whisperings among the older boys,—

"Oh, if Ernest Monroe took the knife, nothing will be said about it. Miss Fosdick is partial to him."

The teacher knew very well what was said; and, though her heart ached sadly, she resolved to treat Ernest exactly as she would have treated his cousin had he been the thief.

CHAPTER VI.

SEARCH FOR THE LIAR.

"I AM more pained than I can express," she said, glancing at the desk where the face of Ernest was hidden on his arms; "but there is still opportunity to confess."

Every breath was hushed, but the sobbing boy did not speak.

"Ernest Monroe," said Miss Fosdick, growing very pale, "rise in your seat."

Ernest obeyed, though his sobs shook his whole frame.

"I have never known you tell a lie. I will trust you now. Did you take my knife from my desk and return it here with a broken blade?"

For one moment Ernest uncovered his face.

"No, ma'am, I never touched your knife; I didn't know it was broken till you showed it to us."

"I believe you," she said, earnestly. "A boy who always has told the truth, deserves to be believed. You may all return to your lessons. Henry Drake, you may remain after school."

It was noticed by all that Henry's face was as red as Ernest's had been.

One of the scholars presently held up his hand for permission to speak to the teacher about his lesson. She went directly to his desk, and, as she passed Henry's seat, she heard him say, in a hurried whisper,—

"If you tell anything about me, Ernest, I'll cut your hand worse than it was before."

Half an hour before school was dismissed, Ernest asked leave to go home, as his head ached badly.

"Yes," was the reply; "and I advise you to lie down till I call, which will be soon after school."

Henry Drake stood before his teacher when school was dismissed, and tried to look careless and indifferent; but she could plainly see marks of guilt.

"Did you take my knife, Henry?" asked the teacher.

"No, ma'am!"

"Don't gaze at the floor now; look me full in the eye. You know there is One who sees into your heart. Can you say, before Him, that you have never touched my knife; that you know nothing how it came broken?"

"I don't see why you want to ask me so many questions," grumbled the boy, beginning to cry. "I told you I didn't know anything about it; but you wont believe me. You wont believe anybody but Ernest."

"I need not tell you, why I can't believe your word, Henry; your own conscience will tell you that. I do believe Ernest, because I know that he loves his Saviour, and would not grieve him by committing so great a sin as to tell a falsehood. If you have done nothing wrong, why did you threaten your cousin, in such a cruel manner, if he told anything about you?"

Henry started, but presently muttered,—

"He's always telling something to get me into trouble."

"No," answered the teacher, "that is not true. Ernest did not tell your father that you stole the keys of his tool chest. He has told me nothing about my knife, though I think that he knows something about it. He was willing to bear all the suspicions of the scholars rather than charge another with the crime. It would be much better for you to confess, Henry. I would forgive you, even now. If, after all your denial, I find you have been the thief and liar, too, I shall make a serious affair of it."

For a moment the boy hesitated. Conscience said, "Confess."

"I got out of the other scrape by sticking to my lie," he said to himself. So he repeated the words,—

"I never touched your knife."

"You may go," said the teacher, sternly. "I don't know whether you have told the truth; but God does. He is a God of truth; and he says all liars shall be punished."

Do you suppose Henry was happy as he walked home? Do you think he whistled, and smiled with pleasant thoughts; that he longed to see his mother and tell her all that had passed? No, he did nothing of all this. He walked slowly, with his head down, wondering, after his threat to Ernest, whether he would dare tell his mother what he knew about the knife.

At last, as he was going into the gate to his own home, he saw Miss Fosdick was just behind him. Without stopping to think what she would imagine, he darted away, and, running into the barn, hid himself among the hay.

CHAPTER VII.

THE UNHAPPY LIAR.

ERNEST was not lying down. He sat in a rocking chair, his head resting on his hand. He smiled when he saw his teacher, and asked her to sit down.

"Mother has gone into Uncle Drake's. She will be back in a minute," he said.

"I came to see you, Ernest. I think, though you haven't touched my knife, you can tell me something about it."

Blushes dyed the boy's cheeks, as he answered,—

"I told mother, and she says ought to tell you."

His lips quivered as he added, "I didn't think you'd believe I had taken it."

"You can never imagine how much pain I felt when I feared temptation had proved too powerful for you. But you see what a good thing it is to be known as a truthful boy. I then believed your word, as I do now."

"I was coming home with Henry," began Ernest, "and I saw him have a beautiful knife. He said he had found it, and was going to keep it. I thought he was telling the truth, till he tried to make me promise not to tell. Then I was afraid there was something wrong. I told him, if he knew whose it was, he ought to carry it back. I didn't see it again till you held it up in school."

"And are you not afraid Henry will carry out his threat, and cut you worse than he did before?"

"Mother has gone in to see Uncle John about that."

"Well, I'm going in there, too. It is time for me to tell his parents what a bad influence he exerts in the school. Unless he repents, and asks forgiveness, I cannot allow him to go back. We must have no thieves nor liars there."

Unfortunately Mr. Drake had gone to a town at some distance, for a load of lumber, and, was not expected home until late. Mrs. Drake invited the teacher into the parlor, and seemed greatly distressed when listening to the account of her son's bad conduct. She said, her husband would be very angry, both with Henry and with her, for keeping from him what she knew about the keys.

Miss Fosdick left a message for Mr. Drake, that Henry could not attend school till he had made a confession of his sin.

When Mr. Monroe came home to supper, and learned the disgraceful story, he started from his chair in great excitement, exclaiming,—

"Henry ought to be sent to the Reform School. If he goes on so, he will come to the gallows. If he dares lay a finger on you, Ernest, I'll have him put there. John may fume and rage as much as he will. I've borne all that I shall from his family."

"Mary Anne feels dreadfully," urged Mrs. Monroe. "I'm so sorry for her sake."

"She'll feel worse yet, Jane, if nothing is done to prevent Henry from acting so shamefully. I yielded to you against my own judgment, and let John believe our Ernest stole his keys. I'll do so no longer."

In the evening, he went over to talk with Mary Anne.

Henry knew that his mother had heard the story of the knife. At the supper-table, the tears trickled down her cheeks, and once she said,—

"O Henry! You'll break my heart if you go on so. Why can't you confess to the teacher, and be a good boy?"

Feeling very restless and unhappy, he went up to his room early; but soon, hearing his uncle's voice, talking in excited tones, he crept softly down to the door where he could hear every word.

"I ought to have done it before," Mr. Monroe was saying. "John has reason to be angry. It isn't doing as I would have him do to me. Henry grows worse every day, and something must be done to correct his dreadful habit of lying."

"I'm afraid John will break every bone in his body," sobbed Mary Anne. "If it hadn't been for that, I should have told him myself about the keys."

"Henry deserves a good thrashing," answered the clock-maker. "It may save him from the gallows. I shall tell John we all knew he was the guilty one, and why I consented to keep it from him for a time. You had better tell him, too."

"I can't! I can't! You don't realize how angry he'll be; and you know he says he'll never forgive."

Henry had heard enough. Trembling from head to foot, he crept back to his chamber; but he did not think of going to bed.

"I'll stay here till mother goes into her room, and then I'll run off. I know there are places enough better than this. At any rate, I wont stay here, where they're all against me, to be half killed by father."

Stealing to the closet, with his bare feet to the floor, he soon discovered his father's pocket-book in the same pocket where the keys had once been, and, taking from it five dollars, all the money it contained, he wrapped it in a paper, and lay down in his clothes.

"I know mother wont tell father a word about it to-night," he said, his teeth chattering, "and I'll be off before he's up. He said he shouldn't be at home till eleven, 'cause the moon wouldn't rise till late; so it will be light for me to run away."

CHAPTER VIII.

THE LIAR REFORMED.

"WHY don't Henry come down to his breakfast?" asked Mr. Drake, in a petulant tone.

"I'll call him now," answered the mother, with a sigh, starting for Henry's chamber.

She saw her brother-in-law coming toward the house, and trembled with fear of her husband's anger.

"You have some excellent lumber out before the shop," remarked Mr. Monroe, coming in and taking his seat.

"I had to give a good deal more for it than it's worth," grumbled the carpenter; "my wheel broke down, too, and I never got home till midnight."

"I'm sorry; but it's most time I was at the factory, and I have something to say to you."

At first Mr. Drake went on eating, as if nothing his brother could say would be worse than his last night's misfortunes. But presently he dropped his knife and fork, his face growing whiter and whiter with rage.

All this time Mrs. Drake had not come down from Henry's chamber, which she had found empty.

Now her husband rose, and going to the foot of the stairs called out,—

"Mary Anne, come down. I want you quick; and if Henry knows what is good for himself, he'll be here in no time."

"Wife," said he, when she came in, looking haggard and frightened at her son's disappearance; "Monroe says you knew all the time that Henry stole the keys from my pocket; that you heard him at it. Is that true?"

"I didn't know what he was going to do with the keys," she said, apologizing.

"And Jane heard Ernest plead with the young scamp, to confess it to me; and he refused because, as he said, I'd half kill him. I was the only one to be deceived,—I, the father of the boy. Well, you'll all see that I am not a man to cover up my child's fault. I'll give Henry the cowhide till he repents of that job."

"Stop," exclaimed Mr. Monroe. "You must know the whole. Lying, as I always said, hardens the heart more than anything else. Henry felt so pleased at not being found out in that thing, that he stole his teacher's knife from her desk, and then, before the whole school, while Ernest was crying for his cousin's fault, he pointed at him as the guilty one. Miss Fosdick heard Henry whisper a threat,—if he dared tell of him, he'd cut him worse than before. There's a boy who must be stopped short in his career, or he will come to an untimely end."

"Henry," called out Mr. Drake, angrily. "Wife, if you're keeping the boy back, it will be the worse for him and for you, too. Tell him to come here this instant."

"I don't know where he is, John. I've been to his room, and he isn't there; and I wont deceive you any more. He's taken all the money out of your pocket-book; I found it empty on the table." And, wholly overcome with her emotions, she fell into a chair, covering her face with her hands.

There was a flash in the father's eye and a paleness about his mouth, as he strode toward the barn to harness his horse, which alarmed Mr. Monroe.

"Brother John," he said, "from the bottom of my heart I pity you. But don't be hasty; don't do anything in your anger that you will be sorry for. Kindness will do more for Henry than anything else. Ask yourself, 'Have I done my duty by my child? Have I taught him as I should?'"

The harness dropped from Mr. Drake's hand, the hardness faded out of the father's face, and, turning to his brother, he said, in a subdued tone,—

"Monroe, you've a right to upbraid me for my harsh talk about Ernest. Why don't you do it? Well, if it's no time now for reproach, when my heart is breaking, I'll take your advice about the boy. Shall I go or stay?"

"Stay, and let him come home. There is no danger of his going far."

Two, three days passed, days of agony to the mother, and of remorse to both. Mr. Drake almost regretted having taken Mr. Monroe's advice, and determined, if nothing was heard from the boy the next day, to start off in search of him.

Late that night, the mother was awakened by a noise under her window. She threw up the sash, when Henry's voice pleaded,—

"O mother! Do let me in. I'm sick and so hungry."

"Lie down, wife; it is better that I should go to him."

Henry shrank back when he saw his father.

"Come in, my poor boy," said the man, putting out his hand, "come in."

He led the wondering child to the stove, where he soon kindled a fire, then went to the closet and brought out the best food it contained.

Henry ate a little and began to cry.

"I'm sorry, father. I'll take the greatest whipping you'll give me, if you'll only let me come home. I stole your keys, and your money, too, and I broke teacher's knife."

"I know it all, my son," said the father. "When I first heard it, I should have whipped you till one of us dropped. I'm glad you was not here. I've forgiven you now, and so has your mother, and poor, abused Ernest. All we want is that you'll begin from this time to be an obedient, truthful boy; and I'll try, with God's help, to be a better father to you than I have ever been before. Now go in and kiss your dear mother, and hurry off to bed."

"Oh, what a load is lifted off my mind!" exclaimed Mr. Drake, when Henry had gone to his chamber. "He's come to his senses, for he confessed right off, and it seems that I have just come to mine."

CHAPTER IX.

CONCLUSION.

THE next day Henry commenced life anew. What do you suppose was the first thing he did? I will tell you. He went to the school, knocked timidly at the door, and told the teacher he wanted to speak to her a minute. There was something in his face which convinced her that he was a penitent boy. So she said kindly,—

"Wait till I dismiss the class in spelling; and I will come to you."

Henry waited nearly ten minutes. I will not deny that he trembled a good deal as he thought of telling her all he had done; and once he said to himself,—

"I can't do it! She'll tell the scholars, and they'll all despise me."

But the remembrance of her kind voice, as she said, "Wait a minute," decided him to remain and bravely confess his guilt.

"I did steal your knife," he exclaimed, as she appeared; "I broke it, too; and then, when it was of no use, I put it back. I didn't feel happy, and that made me cross to Ernest; and I told ever so many lies, and I'm just as sorry as I can be."

The teacher gazed at his eyes, blinded with the big tears he was trying to keep back. She saw that his lip quivered. She heard his broken voice, and she knew that he was really sorry for his sins.

"My dear Henry," she began, "I forgive you heartily, and I feel more encouraged about you now than I ever did before."

Do you think Henry was happy now?

Do you think he refused when she asked him to come in to his seat while she told the school? No, indeed.

And if ever after, he was tempted to lie, he called to mind the dreadful days he had passed away from home, and prayed his heavenly Father to help him always to be an obedient, truthful child.